ORCHARD BOOKS

First published in the USA by Scholastic Inc in 2018
First published in the UK in 2019 by The Watts Publishing Group

7 9 10 8 6

A CIP catalogue record for this book is available from the British Library.

ISBN 978 1 40836 441 3

Printed and bound in Great Britain

MIX
Paper from
responsible sources
FSC® C104740

The paper and board used in this book are
made from wood from responsible sources.

Orchard Books
An imprint of Hachette Children's Group
Part of The Watts Publishing Group Limited
Carmelite House, 50 Victoria Embankment, London EC4Y 0DZ

An Hachette UK Company

www.hachette.co.uk
www.hachettechildrens.co.uk

OLD FRIENDS
NEW BATTLES

Adapted by Jeanette Lane

ORCHARD

CHAPTER 1

CLASS TRIP

"Now, class!" Principal Oak's dark eyes sparkled with excitement. He waited for all the students to pay attention before he continued. "To celebrate the twentieth anniversary of our beloved Pokémon School, we're going on an extra-special field trip."

"Special field trip?!" said Ash Ketchum.

Ash could hardly believe his luck. First of all, he was living in the gorgeous, tropical Alola region and attending the famous Pokémon School. Now that he'd been there for a few months, he felt like a real student, and he claimed all his classmates as friends.

The Pokémon School was like no other. It was a place where people and Pokémon learned together. He and Pikachu fit right in! Principal Oak and Professor Kukui had taught them many new things, especially about the unique Pokémon of the Alola region.

For Ash, the only thing better than going to the Pokémon School was going on a Pokémon School field trip! Ash couldn't wait to hear where they were headed.

"So does that mean we get to go

somewhere amazing?" Mallow wondered.

Ash, Mallow, Sophocles, Lana, Kiawe and Lillie all leaned forward with anticipation.

"We sure do," Professor Kukui answered. He paused before declaring, "We are going to the Kanto region!"

"Oh," Ash mumbled. "Kanto?"

For Ash, Kanto did not seem extra-special or amazing. After all, Kanto was his home

region. He had hoped to travel somewhere new. He wanted to learn more about regional differences of Pokémon, or meet famous Pokémon Trainers.

"You're from the Kanto region, aren't you, Ash?" Kiawe asked. He studied Ash with a serious gaze that was typical Kiawe.

"Yeah," Ash replied, still bummed.

The others didn't feel that way at all. "Professor Oak's world-famous laboratory is there, right?" Sophocles asked, sounding excited.

"Yes, indeed!" Principal Oak declared. "We'll visit my cousin Professor Oak at his laboratory, plus you'll get to see lots of Kanto Pokémon, too!"

"Right, and that's not all," Professor Kukui added. "I want you to have an experience you can't have here, along with some very special guests."

"Special guests? Who are they?" Now Ash was curious. Who were the guests? Did he know them?

"And what can't we do in Alola?" Mallow wondered, twisting one of her long green pigtails. She was adventurous and loved new experiences.

"You'll have to wait until we get there to find out," Professor Kukui said, sounding mysterious.

"Sounds like lots of fun!" Kiawe and Sophocles said at the same time.

"Definitely!" agreed Lana, Lillie and Mallow.

Soon, the whole crew was on its way. Once they were on the plane, Ash had changed his mind. He was going to get to visit home and see his mum!

"I can't wait to get there," Ash said, his own excitement growing. "I'll be able to show you all around." He thought of all the things he'd like to share with his new friends.

"That'll be perfect!" Mallow agreed.

Although returning to the Kanto region wasn't new for Ash, the trip would provide new experiences for his classmates – some more than others.

"Hey, Sophocles! How is this thing flying?!" Kiawe asked nervously as he peered out of the aeroplane window. He took a deep breath in and out, fogging up the glass. It was unusual to see the normally composed and brave Kiawe, proud owner of a Z-Ring, seem so anxious.

Sophocles showed no signs of fear. "As far as I'm concerned," he replied, "it's much safer than a Charizard."

It was clear Kiawe would much prefer to be riding his trusted fire-breathing Pokémon than be trapped inside a machine with metal wings and roaring engines.

Despite Kiawe's concerns, they all landed at the Kanto airport safe and sound. "Here we are!" Ash announced, already seeing familiar sights as they walked through the airport.

"I hope we get to see a Vileplume!" Mallow said.

"Horsea and Seadra, too!" Lana added, focusing on her favourite Water-type Pokémon.

Everyone was looking forward to the coming adventure, except Lillie.

"Oh no. Is something wrong, Snowy?" Lillie asked, leaning over her beloved Pokémon. She could tell something wasn't right. Her Alolan Vulpix looked tired and droopy. Even its tail looked less fluffy. "Don't you feel well? Poor dear ..." Snowy collapsed in her arms. "Now what should I do?"

Lillie was a worrier by nature. Even

though she had read hundreds of books about Pokémon over the years, she was not sure how to handle certain situations. And they were in a new, foreign place. What was Lillie going to do?

CHAPTER 2

OLD FRIENDS

Lillie looked around. The rest of the
Pokémon School group had moved on.
Lillie rubbed Snowy's soft head and
mumbled to herself. She wasn't sure what
to do.

"Excuse me," said a stranger with a low
voice and a thick crop of dark hair. "Your

Vulpix, would you mind if I examine it?"
He carried a medical bag. "See, I'm actually
studying to become a Pokémon Doctor."

Lillie let out a sigh of relief. "That would
be great! We got off the plane, then all of a
sudden ..." Lillie's voice faltered
with concern.

"Leave it to me." The stranger seemed
very confident and he looked trustworthy

in his waistcoat with many pockets. He carefully examined Snowy, who let out weak moans now and again.

Of course, Lillie had no way of knowing that the stranger was not a stranger to Ash. It was his old friend and travelling companion, Brock!

Meanwhile, some other familiar faces had also recently arrived from Alola. They were not exactly strangers, but they weren't friends either. Team Rocket were in the Kanto airport and they were all in a bad mood, as always.

"Ugh, this is so depressing," Jessie complained.

"Going through all of this to get to headquarters," James continued. They were annoyed.

"Why do we have to take orders from

that girl with the bob haircut and wire-rimmed glasses, anyway?!" Meowth wondered out loud.

Jessie, James and Meowth were frustrated with the fact that their boss had someone new working for him. What was even worse was that the new person seemed to think the members of Team Rocket worked for her. Jessie, James and Meowth hated her attitude.

"If we don't follow her orders, we'll get more lectures than in all my school years combined!" James whined.

"Hey, don't worry," Meowth said. "If we give Loser Locks this yummy pastry, she's sure to be in a good mood!" Meowth held up a sticky bun in hopes that it would be a good bribe, but then he frowned. "Yeah, like that's gonna work."

The airport was so crowded, no one from the Pokémon School noticed Jessie, James and Meowth.

Lillie, especially, did not notice them. She was too focused on Snowy.

"Just as I suspected," Brock said. "A little airsickness." He put the stethoscope back in his medical kit.

"Oh, thank you very much!" Lillie said, snuggling with her Vulpix.

"I wonder where Lillie is," Mallow said to Ash.

Ash glanced around. He spotted Lillie and then he noticed she was talking to someone. Ash would recognise that figure anywhere!

"Is that Brock?!" he wondered out loud. "Heyyyy! Brock!" he shouted, racing straight for his old friend.

Brock looked up but he didn't seem to notice Ash. He'd spotted a young flight attendant. "Wow!" He ran past Ash and stopped in front of the young woman. "Ahh … wouldn't it be paradise if we flew the lovely skies together!"

Brock was infamous for falling in love fast. He began one of his trademark love poems, pulling a bouquet of roses out of nowhere and presenting them to the flight attendant.

"Chasing clouds with you … Soaring on love's wing …"

Brock sounded very devoted – until someone started to pull his earlobe. "Ow, ow, ow, ow, ow … OW!" he yelped.

"Really? I come all the way to pick you up at the airport, and this is the thanks I get?!" said the person pulling on Brock's ear.

"Ha! Misty!" Ash could hardly believe it. It was his old friend Misty pinching Brock's ear! Ash's two original travelling companions were in the airport.

"Hey, Ash!" Misty said with a friendly wave. She wore the same jean shorts, red braces and cute, lopsided ponytail as always. "How have you been?"

Pikachu was so excited, it bounded right off Ash's shoulder and into Misty's arms.

Releasing her hold on Brock's earlobe, Misty gave Pikachu a big hug. "Long time no see, Pikachu!" she greeted the affectionate Pokémon with a giggle.

From behind a nearby pillar, Team Rocket watched the reunion of their longtime enemies. "It's the original Twerp, Twerp and Twerpette trio!" Jessie moaned.

"What are they doing here?" James asked,

his eyes narrowing.

"Let me introduce you," Ash said, turning to his Pokémon School classmates. "These are my friends, and we travelled together before."

"Nice to meet you. I'm Misty, internationally known beauty," said Misty. "I'm also the Cerulean City Gym Leader!"

"You're a Gym Leader?" Mallow's voice

was full of admiration.

"And an … internationally known beauty?" Lana asked.

"I'm Brock! A Pokémon Breeder as well as a Pokémon doctor in training. I'm also the former Pewter City Gym Leader," Brock explained. "The pleasure to meet you is mine, all mine."

"Hi there, Brock. My name's Sophocles!" Sophocles, like many of the students, held his favourite Pokémon in his arms. Togedemaru chirped a hello as well.

"I'm Lillie."

"I'm Kiawe."

"My name's Mallow!"

"And I'm Lana." From its perch on Lana's head, Popplio waved a friendly fin.

"What are you two doing here?" Ash asked, looking from Misty to Brock.

"Well, Professor Oak asked us to come," Misty admitted.

Ash nodded. "So you must be the special guests!"

"Hold on!" Professor Kukui called out. "We'll get to the truth and quash any rumours when we're on the road!"

"Right, my cousin is waiting. Shellos we go?" Principal Oak said. He loved using Pokémon names as puns.

Team Rocket had been just close enough to eavesdrop on the whole conversation. "Sounds like they're on their way to Professor Oak's lab," Jessie pointed out with a scowl.

"That place is the picture-perfect place to pick a pile of primo Pokémon!" Meowth proclaimed. The Normal-type Pokémon was always thinking ahead.

"I predict if we catch them all and present those Pokémon to the boss, it will be lecture over and class dismissed!" Jessie said, hatching a plan to get back on the boss's good side.

"Wobbuffet!" Wobbuffet, an often-silent member of Team Rocket, announced its approval.

Jessie was right. If Team Rocket could

infiltrate the grounds of Professor Oak's Lab, they might be able to steal some of the best-trained and most powerful Pokémon of all time – Pikachu, Turtonator, Popplio, Steenee, Togedemaru and so many more.

But would Team Rocket's plan to steal all the Pokémon School students' best battle partners actually work?

CHAPTER 3

AT THE LABORATORY

After a short drive past rolling meadows, tall forests and clear rivers, the crew arrived at Professor Oak's famous Pokémon Laboratory. With its plum-coloured roof and tall windmill, it was quite a landmark. While Ash had been there many times before, his classmates were in awe.

"Samson!" Professor Oak called out as everyone entered the Laboratory.

"Dear Samuel!" Principal Oak returned the greeting, grabbing his cousin's hand and giving it a firm, friendly shake.

"Congratulations on the twentieth anniversary of your Pokémon School!" Professor Oak said.

"Thanks, cousin!"

"They're the same!" Rotom Dex cried out. It hovered between the two cousins, calculating each one's appearance. "Except for their hair, their other features – like their noses and mouths – are a ninety-nine point nine per cent match!"

It was true! Principal Oak had long grey hair and wore a short-sleeved tropical shirt. The professor had shorter, light-brown hair and wore a buttoned shirt and white lab coat, but the two men still looked very much alike.

"Everyone! This is my dear cousin and the world's leading authority on Pokémon research," the principal announced to his students. "Let me present Professor Samuel Oak!"

"Ahem." Professor Oak cleared his throat. "And now I believe it is time for a Pokémon poem." He paused before reciting his lines.

"Twenty years.

How Bulbizarre the passing of time

can be,

Catching Pokémon for everyone to see!"

The principal, Professor Kukui and the
Pokémon School students all clapped. Even
Popplio flapped its fins together.

"Here's one of my poems for you!"
Rotom Dex said. It went up to
Principal Oak and Professor Oak and
recited its poem right next to the cousins.

"Same faces,

side by side.

A Bulbizarre ride!"

"Brilliantly done!" Principal Oak and
Professor Oak announced in unison.

"Poetry's fun!" Rotom agreed.

Next, Professor Oak invited everyone to

take a long tour of the Pokémon Laboratory grounds. "I've asked Brock and Misty to be your guides," he said. "I know they'll be great!"

"Thanks!" Brock replied.

"We won't let you down!" Misty assured them.

"Whoa," Mallow and Kiawe said together as they stepped outside through double doors.

"It's huge!" Sophocles observed as he took in the lush green fields, tree-covered hills and vast blue sky. There was a fenced-in area, a large barn and lots of space for Pokémon to roam free.

"And so many Pokémon, too!" said Lillie. She could see such a variety of Pokémon milling around the grounds, including

Exeggcute, Bellsprout, Chansey and more.

"I know!" Ash agreed.

"Some of these Pokémon have Trainers who asked us to care for them while they're gone," Brock told the group. "Some are Pokémon we've taken in. And some are wild Pokémon who just showed up."

"No time to waste, so let's go and see them!" Misty said.

"This is the perfect place to gather Pokémon data!" Rotom Dex was in heaven! It had so much new data to collect on Kanto Pokémon.

Sophocles glanced around. "I want to see a Kanto Raichu!" he said.

"When I think of Kanto," Kiawe said, "it's got to be Fire-type Pokémon." Kiawe had no problem admitting he had a favourite type.

Lana repeated her own wishes for Kanto

sightings. "Horsea! Seadra!"

"There are so many Pokémon I want to see …" said Lillie. "Oh, look! Ooh, a Spearow!"

"We have them in Alola, too," Mallow pointed out.

"I guess you're right," Lillie admitted with an embarrassed grin. She just adored all Pokémon.

"A lot of my Pokémon are living here, too," Ash said. "There they are!" He pointed across a long flat field to a herd of large Wild Bull Pokémon. "Hey! Look, Tauros, it's me!"

At once, the Pokémon stopped grazing and looked in the direction of the small school group. Ash rushed out, excited to be reunited with his Pokémon. But the whole herd began to stampede towards him, hooves pounding the ground.

Ash didn't look very concerned, but his friends were!

"What's going on?!" Mallow cried, her hands held up to her face in shock.

"What's Ash doing?!" Sophocles said, asking the question they were all wondering.

"Tauros!" Ash yelled as they grew near, but the Wild Bull Pokémon were going too fast to slow down. Even Pikachu grew alarmed as one of the Tauros hit Ash head-on, and the young Pokémon Trainer was tossed high into the sky.

Luckily, Ash wasn't hurt, but that was the last time he'd ever yell to a whole herd of Pokémon with moves like Zen Headbutt, Horn Attack and Giga Impact!

CHAPTER 4

KANTO POKÉMON

There was so much to see in Kanto! It was hard to stay together because everyone wanted to investigate different new and exciting Pokémon.

Kiawe wandered away from the group, taking in the beautiful surroundings. He came to a grassy ridge and noticed a majestic Pokémon standing at the top.

"Wow! That's—"

"Rapidash," Rotom Dex finished Kiawe's sentence. "The Fire Horse Pokémon. A Fire-type. Rapidash loves to gallop. Whenever it sees something moving fast, it gets the urge to race."

Kiawe knew another Pokémon who loved to race! He watched Rapidash run down a dirt bank to a grassy field. The Fire Horse Pokémon looked so at ease as it galloped. It grew faster with each stride, its mane and tail streaming behind it like a wild flame.

Kiawe was amazed. "All right! Charizard, let's go!" he yelled. He tossed a Poké Ball and his own Flame Pokémon appeared.

"Ready to fly?" Kiawe asked.

Charizard took off with a mighty flap of its wings. Soon, the Pokémon and Trainer

were soaring right behind the Fire Horse
Pokémon. "Want to have a race, Rapidash?"

With a giddy snort, Rapidash accepted the
challenge. It burst ahead with new speed.

Charizard soared just above the galloping
Pokémon. They kept pace with each other.
Rapidash threw its head in the air and
whinnied to Kiawe.

"Really?" Kiawe asked. "You want me to
hop on?"

Carefully, Kiawe leaned over Charizard's side and landed on Rapidash's back. Almost immediately, he yelped. The Pokémon's mane was on fire!

"I'm in awe!" he said, thrilled.

"Kiawe! How far are you going?" Rotom Dex called out. There was concern in its voice, but Kiawe didn't even look back.

Not far away, the other Pokémon School students were encountering more Pokémon from the Kanto region.

"So this is a Vileplume for real!" Mallow declared. "And a pair of Gloom, too! Alola, cuties!" She leaned over to get a closer look at the colourful Flower Pokémon and the Weed Pokémon.

"Vileplume's pollen is poisonous!" Brock warned from a distance.

Unfortunately, Mallow didn't hear him.

A cloud of sparkly purple pollen burst from Vileplume's top.

"Get away! Get away! Get away! GET AWAY!" Misty and Brock yelled at the top of their voices, waving their arms. "It's poisonous!"

"Nooooo!" Mallow screeched. She scooped up Steenee and darted away as fast

as her legs would carry her.

Sophocles was on a mission of his own. "Found it!" he declared, parting the leaves in a group of tall bushes. He had tracked down a Kanto Raichu!

Togedemaru seemed just as excited as Sophocles. The friendly little Pokémon rushed forward and raced circles around Raichu. It ran so fast that it created an electric charge that zapped Raichu! Raichu's head buzzed as it toppled over.

"Are you OK?" Sophocles asked, hurrying up to the fallen Raichu. Luckily, it was just stunned and it seemed to be in a happy, drowsy state.

Lillie and Snowy had a much sweeter meeting with a new friend. "Snowy, that Pokémon is a Ninetales from Kanto," Lillie said.

Snowy slowly approached the regal

Fox Pokémon. Ninetales gave the
Alolan Vulpix a lick.

Lillie was a true student of all Pokémon,
but she was especially interested in the
Kanto region's evolved form of Vulpix. With
its red eyes, the Fire-type Pokémon was truly
mesmerising.

"What a cute Pokémon!" Lana said when
she and Popplio encountered a Dewgong.
The Water- and Ice-type Pokémon was
especially playful.

Pikachu and Ash were thrilled to see their
friends from the Alola region enjoying the
field trip so much.

"Coming to Kanto with everybody sure
is fun!" Ash declared. "Hold on," he said,
looking around. "Where did Rotom go?"

Of course, Rotom Dex was probably
having the most fun of all. It was on a

mission to record all Pokémon everywhere and the visit to Kanto presented so many opportunities to update data!

"If I keep this up, I'll be able to complete my data covering every Pokémon in Kanto!" Rotom Dex said.

"Now, check these out," Brock directed when the group was all back together. He and Misty each tossed a Poké Ball in the same direction.

"Notice any differences?" Brock asked when two Pokémon appeared.

Exeggutor from Kanto and Exeggutor from Alola were side by side. They seemed shocked to be standing next to each other, grumbling as they looked around.

The students from the Pokémon School were amazed. It was one thing to study the regional differences in Pokémon, but it was pretty awesome to compare the two side by side, right there on the grounds of Professor Oak's Pokémon Laboratory.

"Kanto's Exeggutor is so short," Lana observed.

"I guess it doesn't get as much sun here," Kiawe commented.

"They're different, all right," Mallow said.

Alolan Exeggutor had a long, thick

neck that swayed like a palm tree. Kanto Exeggutor's neck was so stubby, it was hard to see. But they both had three round heads, with sharp fangs and googly eyes. They both also had long tufts of grass that grew like hair.

"Here are my partners!" Brock said as he tossed two more Poké Balls. Two different Geodude appeared, both flexing their arm muscles.

Still, there were differences.

"That Geodude has no eyebrows," Lana pointed out.

"Are you saying those are eyebrows?" Sophocles asked.

Next, they compared a Muk from Alola to a Muk from Kanto.

"Muk, it's good to see you again ..." Ash said, as his own Muk embraced him in a

smelly, gunky hug.

"Last but not least …" Brock said and a Kanto Marowak popped out of a Poké Ball.

"I present you with Alolan Marowak!" Kiawe said, throwing his own Poké Ball.

Immediately, the two Marowak butted heads and started spinning the bones each was carrying.

"Hey, cut it out!" Kiawe yelled.

"Come on, no fighting!" Brock scolded, but the two Marowak continued to face off. Brock and Kiawe had to hold them back.

"Their short-tempered personalities are the same," Mallow noted.

"Yeah, but I think their types are different," Sophocles said.

"You're right," Kiawe agreed. "My Marowak is a Fire- and Ghost-type."

"I know I read that the Kanto Marowak is a Ground type," said Lillie.

"Correct. I'm impressed!" said Brock.

Meanwhile, Pikachu was trying to separate the two Bone Keeper Pokémon, but they lashed out and sent Pikachu flying.

Next, Togedemaru tried to butt in and soon it was a messy battle, with everyone chasing one another.

As soon as Pikachu was back on its feet, it

stepped in. The Mouse Pokémon let out a massive, frustrated blast, sending an intense electric jolt through all the Pokémon and Trainers. Everyone was stunned!

CHAPTER 5

MISSING POKÉMON

After they had all recovered from Pikachu's move, Lana realised something was wrong. "Popplio's missing!" she called out.

"Marowak's missing, too!" Kiawe said.

"They're GONE?!" Brock said in surprise.

Soon, all the Trainers had begun to search. Ash, Misty and Brock looked together, walking along a wooded path.

"Popplio?" Ash called.

"Marowak?" yelled Brock.

"Where are you?" wondered Misty.

"Pika, pika?" Pikachu heard a rustling nearby.

Just then, a Caterpie wriggled out from behind a bush.

"You'd better stay away from me!" Misty shrieked, running to hide behind a tree.

Ash swallowed a laugh. "Some things stay the same," he said, shaking his head. "You're still scared of Bug-type Pokémon?" he asked Misty.

"Bug-type Pokémon bug me more than I can say," Misty confessed, peeking out from behind the tree trunk.

"Misty, you sure haven't changed a bit," Ash said as they went back to searching.

"Brings back memories," Brock added. "I mean, of how the three of us used to travel together. We did lots of things and had lots of fun!"

"Although not everything was fun," Misty replied thoughtfully.

"I enjoyed every moment of our journey," Ash told his friends.

"I'm a little jealous of how carefree you are," Misty told Ash. While Ash was

still travelling the world on his Pokémon adventure, Misty had the big responsibility of being a Gym Leader.

Suddenly, they heard voices from deep among the trees. "What was that?" Ash cried.

"Let's see!" said Brock.

The friends crept into the forest. When they came to a clearing, they saw a group of Pokémon having a disagreement.

"It's Bulbasaur!" Ash cried with joy when he saw that his beloved Grass- and Poison-type Pokémon was among them.

"Bul-ba-saur!" The Seed Pokémon was overjoyed.

"How have you been?" Ash asked as Bulbasaur scampered over and bounded into his arms.

"Bul-ba-saur, saur, saur, saur," Bulbasaur

replied, nuzzling up to Ash.

"Pika, pi!" Pikachu was happy to see its old buddy, too.

"It's been a long time," Brock said, watching the three cuddle. "Bulbasaur's thrilled!"

"Isn't it great?" Misty agreed.

After a while, Misty left Ash and Brock and ran to find Lana, Lillie and Mallow.

They were still looking for Popplio.

"Hey, guys!" Misty greeted them. "Still haven't found Popplio yet?"

"No," Lana replied, sounding bewildered. The others could hear the concern in her voice.

"There's a lake up ahead. I think we should check it out," Misty suggested. As always, she was upbeat and happy to lend a hand.

Misty led them to a bluff overlooking a clear blue lake.

"Maybe Popplio is playing in the water," Lana said hopefully, leaning down.

Just then, a Gyarados reared out of the water with a tremendous splash. The Atrocious Pokémon opened its mouth and let out a ferocious roar.

"Ahhhh!" Mallow, Lillie and Misty cried.

They quickly ran away.

But Lana was not scared at all. "I'll take a look," she said, shedding her clothes to reveal a sleek blue swimsuit. She dived straight into the water.

When Misty realised Lana had plunged in, she turned back around.

"Lana's brave," Misty said. "Well, she's not the only one who's brave! So I'm going to be brave, too!"

Misty dived into the water and both Trainers swam deeper, searching for Popplio. They passed Poliwag, Magikarp and other Water-type Pokémon.

It wasn't long before they found Popplio resting on the bottom of the lake with a Slowpoke and two Horsea.

Back on land, Ash and the others were still trying to track down Marowak.

"I know how Marowak gets. I hope it's not in a fight somewhere," Kiawe worried out loud.

"All right, then," Sophocles said, pulling a tiny gadget from his pocket. "I'll use this software I programmed—"

But as he spoke, the ground beneath him began to shake. With a loud rumble, Onix,

the Rock Snake Pokémon, emerged from the craggy ground. It was gigantic, the size of a train!

"Let's do it, Turtonator!" Kiawe called out.

Kiawe had already thrown his Poké Ball when Brock held out his arms to stop him. "Just stay calm," Brock advised, his voice even. "As long as we do that, we'll be fine."

Ash, Sophocles, Kiawe and their Pokémon

held their breaths.

Onix quietened down and lowered its immense grey head to take a better look at the group. When it gave a gentle grunt and looked away, the Trainers all let out a sigh of relief.

Unfortunately, that was the same moment Marowak reappeared and threw its bone right in Onix's face.

"Marowak!" it yelled like a battle cry.

"I guess you wouldn't call that staying calm, right, Brock?" Kiawe admitted, holding back his frustration.

"You know what I'd say?" Brock replied. "Run!"

Everyone – Brock, Ash, Pikachu, Sophocles, Kiawe, Marowak and Turtonator – raced away at full speed!

Onix crashed and slithered behind them.

It chased them deeper into the forest until they finally lost the Pokémon and found the rest of the Pokémon School group.

CHAPTER 6

TEAM ROCKET

"At least it's a big relief that we found everybody," said Ash as he looked around at the group. They were deep in the forest now. If Ash was right, they weren't very far from his house.

They had all met lots of friendly new Pokémon. Popplio and Marowak had gone missing. The girls had encountered a Gyarados, and the boys had a meeting with an Onix. It had been an eventful day!

But as soon as the whole gang was back together, a giant net swooped down, trapped all the Pokémon and dragged them into the open hatch of a giant robot!

"What's that?!" Ash asked, instantly worried about Pikachu and the others. He

looked at the tall metal creature, which resembled ... Meowth!

Ash's answer came in the form of a battle poem – Team Rocket style.

"Prepare for trouble, like twerps used to do!

And make it double; we'll put a spell on you!

To protect the world from devastation!

To unite all people within our nation!

To denounce the evils of truth and love!

To extend our reach to the stars above!

Jessie!

James!

Team Rocket, yours truly, blasts off at the speed of light!

Surrender now or prepare yourselves for a sentimental fight!

Meowth, that's right!

Wobbuffet!"

"Team Rocket!" Ash shouted. He realised that Jessie, James, Meowth and Wobbuffet must be inside the giant robot – the robot that was shaped like a huge, frightening Meowth!

Ash could hardly believe that the pesky members of Team Rocket were in Kanto, too! Then again, Team Rocket had a weird habit of showing up wherever Ash and Pikachu happened to be.

"By now, you'd think they would have given it up!" Misty said, not at all surprised to run into their old enemies.

"Give everyone's Pokémon back!" Brock demanded.

"You may be an original Twerp," Jessie told him from inside the robot, "but you're certainly not the best!"

"They're our Pokémon now," James

added, "so give it a rest."

The robot lifted its steel foot and stomped down with a clank. The ground quaked.

"Some things never change," Ash said, knowing they'd have to battle. "OK, Lycanroc, I choose you!"

At once, Lycanroc, the Wolf Pokémon, appeared.

"Use Rock Throw!" Ash directed, and

Lycanroc sent a flurry of rocks flying.

"Rock my Robo-Meowth Mash!" Meowth replied, and an assault shot out from the Team Rocket robot's paw. The Pokémon School crew ducked for cover.

"Just like old times," Brock said, pulling out a Poké Ball. "Crobat, go!"

"Ready, steady … come on out!" Misty shouted and Staryu appeared.

"Now, Lycanroc, Accelerock!" Ash cried.

Lycanroc sprang forward and hit the robot square in the chest.

"The NERVE!" Meowth cried, disgusted. "I'll teach you twerps a lesson!"

"Now, Crobat!" Brock directed. "Supersonic!"

Crobat focused its beam at the robot's paw just as Meowth was going to shoot another attack.

Meowth screeched in anger. "My paw won't work!" he cried. "What a jerk!"

Misty commanded Staryu to use Bubble Beam and the Star Shape Pokémon shot a stream of bubbles at the robot – right where the net had dragged in all the kidnapped Pokémon! Staryu's beam kept pounding at the robot until the hatch popped open and everyone's Pokémon burst out on to the forest floor.

"Pikachu!" Ash yelled happily as the Mouse Pokémon jumped into his arms.

The giant Meowth robot began to crackle and crumble, its circuits sparking. Even as the robot smashed to the ground, its mouth opened and Team Rocket appeared, unscathed.

"Didn't feel a thing," James declared, standing ready for another battle.

"Rise and shine, Mimikyu," Jessie demanded, throwing a Poké Ball.

But before she could tell Mimikyu how to attack, something fell from the sky above and landed in the forest clearing in a cloud of dust.

Ash recognised it at once. It was Bewear, the Strong Arm Pokémon from Alola. It was the same Bewear that had been hounding

Team Rocket since they'd arrived in the tropical paradise. Now Bewear was in some kind of rocket, and it gathered Team Rocket in its strong arms and jetted up into the air.

"And it's liftoff with a new blast!" Team Rocket exclaimed with a sigh.

Ash, Misty, Brock and their friends from the Pokémon School watched as Bewear and Team Rocket zoomed away.

"Anybody know what just happened?" Misty asked in disbelief.

"Don't look at me," Brock insisted.

Ash was about to explain, but then they all heard someone call out, "Ash!"

Ash would recognise that voice anywhere. It was his mum, Delia. He had missed her!

"Hey, Mum!" he called out, running towards her.

"Everything's all set for your welcome

home party!" she assured him.

Ash knew his mother would throw a wonderful gathering for him and all his friends – new and old. Also, he realised that he was extremely hungry!

A little later, everyone was eating and talking and enjoying themselves.

"To reunions!" Professor Oak toasted.

"To reunions!" everyone responded.

"Welcome to Pallet Town, dears," Ash's mum said, looking around. "I hope you have time to see everything." She held Litten in her arms and the Fire Cat Pokémon had never looked more content. It gave a happy purr.

"We will," Kiawe and Sophocles answered with certainty.

"If you want to see a complete mess, you should see Ash's room," Delia joked.

"Hey, Mum, stop it!" Ash begged, feeling embarrassed. He was happy when Rotom Dex flew by to distract everyone.

"What's the matter, Rotom?" Ash asked, seeing the device's frown. "Where have you been?"

"I can't find the last Pokémon to complete my Kanto Pokémon database," Rotom Dex complained. "Frustrating!" It had been busy all day, collecting information non-stop. How could it have missed one of Kanto's Pokémon?

While Alola had the allure of the many Island Guardians, Kanto had its own mysteries, too. Not far away, the Mythical Pokémon Mew watched the gathering at Ash's house. Mew, a Psychic-type Pokémon,

had the ability to turn invisible to keep others from noticing it.

Mew floated away quietly into the deep woods, and Rotom would never even know that it had been so close.

After everyone had eaten and talked for a while, Professor Kukui stood up to thank their hostess. Ash's mum looked happy to have everyone there – especially Ash.

Professor Kukui wanted to talk about his lesson plan for the next day.

"Awesome!" Ash said, ready for anything. "What are we gonna do?"

"We're going to Quick Attack our way to battle at the Cerulean City Gym!" said Professor Kukui.

"Really?" Lana asked.

"At the Cerulean City Gym?" Mallow said, her voice filled with awe.

"Yup, that's right," Misty confirmed. "You are all going to battle at my Gym!"

"We're going to compete in a Gym battle ..." Kiawe said to himself thoughtfully.

"I'm getting fired up!" Ash exclaimed. It had been a long time since he had been in a Gym battle, and what better place than Kanto to get back in the game!

CHAPTER 7

READY FOR BATTLE

After a good night's sleep, Ash woke up anxious. That day he would have a chance to compete in a Gym battle again – against Brock or Misty!

"Oh, YEAH!" Ash said as he and his friends rode toward the Cerulean City Gym.

The whole Pokémon School crew was

in awe as they scrambled off the bus and walked towards the entrance. It was an enormous building with a glass roof that looked a lot like a cut diamond – a Gym that looked like a gem!

"Look!" Sophocles pointed out once they were inside. "Something's over there!"

There was "something" standing in the middle of the arena, not moving.

"Hey, it's Psyduck!" Ash said. Psyduck had always been one of Misty's favourites, even if it was a little unpredictable.

"Pika, pika!" Of course Pikachu remembered Psyduck. Psyduck was unforgettable!

"So cute!" Lana said of the Water-type Pokémon.

"Hey!" Misty said, entering the arena. "Thanks a lot for keeping an eye out, Psyduck!" She turned around and greeted her guests. "Welcome to Cerulean City Gym. My Gym!"

"Yeah! It's been so long since I've felt like this," Ash announced. "I want to start battling right away!"

Professor Kukui stepped forwards, not wanting Ash to get ahead of himself. "You all remember Misty and Brock," he

said. "Misty is the leader of the Cerulean City Gym and an expert on Water-type Pokémon."

"Nice to see you all!" Misty said.

"And Brock is the former Pewter City Gym Leader and a Rock-type Pokémon expert," Professor Kukui declared.

"Hey there!" Brock said with a casual wave.

"These are the two you'll be battling!

I want you all to feel the heat! It's like a Blast Burn!" said Professor Kukui.

Feel the heat? Ash thought that was a funny line coming from Professor Kukui. After all, everyone knew that the Alola region was much hotter than Kanto.

Still, Ash had a good feeling about battling today. First of all, he had been right! Misty and Brock were the special guests that Principal Oak and Professor Kukui had talked about. Second of all, Ash knew Misty and Brock well. They would play fair and help the Pokémon School students learn about Gym battles, but they would also bring their best skills. It was going to be awesome!

"Pokémon Trainers in the Kanto region make their way from Gym to Gym while battling the Gym Leaders," Professor Kukui explained. "A Trainer who wins this battle receives a Gym badge as proof of victory."

Just hearing those words brought back so many memories for Ash. While he still had the same goal of becoming a Pokémon Master, a lot of other things had changed since his time in Kanto.

"The Cerulean City Gym has the Cascade Badge," Misty announced, holding up a badge that looked like a raindrop.

"And this is proof of victory at the Pewter City Gym," Brock said, holding out a shiny metal medallion. "The Boulder Badge!"

"Pretty, huh?" Lillie said. Lana agreed.

The Pokémon School students were all excited, but Ash knew the truth. His old friends were not just going to give those badges away. If the students wanted a Gym badge, they'd have to earn it.

"You won all the badges from the Kanto region, right?" Kiawe said to Ash.

"Sure did!" Ash replied. "You can win eight badges and I won them all!"

Pikachu looked at Ash, uncertain.

"In my case, I gave him a badge out of pity," Misty told them with chuckle.

"Say, that story has a familiar ring," Brock added with a sly grin.

"What's going on?" Kiawe asked Ash. "What do they mean?"

Looking sheepish, Ash quickly changed the subject. "After you've collected all eight badges, you compete in the Pokémon League!"

"The Pokémon League?" Mallow repeated, interested.

"It's a big tournament where the best Trainers compete against one another!" Ash explained, making it sound very grand.

"Pika?" Pikachu gave Ash another questioning look.

"So why don't we start right off with some practice battles against Misty and Brock," Professor Kukui suggested. "Which of you lucky Trainers is up first?"

Everyone raised their hands at once and yelled, "Me!"

"I want to battle Misty!" Lana announced.

"OK, you're in!" said Misty.

"Please?" begged Mallow. "One more?"

"I'd rather battle against Brock," Sophocles said.

"Me too," Kiawe agreed. With his Fire-type Pokémon, Kiawe assumed he'd have a better chance against a Trainer who specialised in Rock-type Pokémon.

"I wanna battle both of them!" Ash declared.

"Oh dear," Lillie said. "How do I choose?"

"Please don't worry," Misty said with a laugh. "It'll be fine. Now, ready to go?"

Lana and Mallow took their positions.

"Hey, guys!" Ash yelled. "Misty may not look it, but she's tough! Give it all you've got!"

"What do you mean by that, Ash? I look

tough enough," Misty objected. "OK, gang. Let's see what you can do!"

"I'll make sure to record all the action!" Rotom Dex promised, and everyone prepared to watch the first practice battle.

CHAPTER 8

FIRST GYM BATTLES

"I'm all set to go!" Mallow declared. She looked at Lana to make sure she was also ready for their battle with Misty, the Cerulean City Gym Leader.

"All right, Steenee, Magical Leaf!" Mallow directed.

"Stee-nee, stee-nee!" The Fruit Pokémon

created a vibrant green burst of glowing leaves that whooshed towards, and twirled all around, Psyduck.

"Popplio, use Bubble Beam!" Lana commanded. The Sea Lion Pokémon blasted tiny bubbles at Psyduck, bowling it over.

Psyduck lay on the arena ground, its webbed feet flailing in the air.

"All right!" Lana cheered.

"I think we won!" Mallow said with glee.

"Psyduck, use Water Gun!" Misty said, unfazed. A moment later, Psyduck was up and shooting a thick stream of water right at Popplio.

The Sea Lion Pokémon blew a bubble that gathered up all the water. The bubble grew and grew and grew. Popplio balanced it on its tiny pink nose like an oversized balloon.

"You're kidding!" Misty said, impressed.

"Popplio, that was great!" Lana told her battle partner.

"Popplio sucked in all the water!" Sophocles murmured, amazed.

"Lana, that was pretty creative!" Misty admitted. "So what do you do with it?"

"Balloon Launch!" Lana called, and Popplio bounced the bubble in the air.

Then, with a flip of its tail, it rolled the bubble at Psyduck. It rolled over Psyduck, trapping it inside. Then the bubble floated high in the air, taking Psyduck with it.

"When Lana and Popplio start their balloon work, they're simply amazing!" Mallow cheered.

"Yeah, they are. But you should know Psyduck is at its best when the chips are down," Misty told them. "Use Confusion!"

Psyduck grabbed its head and blinked again and again, trying to focus.

"Psyduck?" Misty said.

"Why isn't Psyduck using the move?" Rotom asked.

"Because Misty's Psyduck is kind of a flake," Ash told them.

"Use Magical Leaf one more time," Mallow said to Steenee.

"Stee-nee!" The glowing leaves hit the floating balloon head-on and it burst. Psyduck fell straight down to the ground, landing on its head.

Mallow cringed when she saw Psyduck crash down. "Sorry about that!" she said.

"That's going to leave a mark," said Lana.

"Psyduck will be fine," Misty assured them. "No worries!"

Psyduck looked pained … and a little bewildered.

"Here it comes," warned Misty.

Pikachu watched, holding its breath.

All at once, Psyduck's expression changed. It grasped its head harder, shaking. Its eyes shot blue Confusion waves at Steenee and Popplio, stunning them and lifting them right up in the air.

"That's Confusion," Sophocles pointed

out. "Why use that now?"

It didn't matter that the Confusion move had come late in the match. The attack had knocked Steenee and Popplio out of the battle.

"Yeah, that's enough," Misty called to Psyduck. "Great! I think it's time to let Steenee and Popplio down now."

"And that's that," Professor Kukui announced. "They're done."

"I always knew Misty and Psyduck made a great team!" Ash exclaimed.

"Thanks," Misty said, hugging the Duck Pokémon. "Psyduck is such a sweetheart." She stood up and faced her opponents. "You two have shown great battle instincts," Misty told Mallow and Lana with a smile.

"Oh, go on," Mallow responded, happy to get the compliment.

"I feel more confident already," Lana
admitted.

"Now!" Brock called out to Lillie and
Sophocles. "Time for our battle!"

"Geodude!" Brock's battle partner for the
match was Geodude, the Rock Pokémon.

"Right! Togedemaru!" Sophocles shouted,
raising his fist. "Zing Zap, let's go!"

Togedemaru lit up with an electrical
charge and rolled right at Geodude.

It made a solid hit on the Rock Pokémon, but Geodude just flexed its muscles and grinned.

"But how?" Sophocles questioned. "It didn't do a thing!"

"You're right," agreed Lillie.

"Why not?! Electric-type moves should have some effect! Geodude's a Rock- and Electric-type Pokémon!"

"But I think you're talking about an Alolan Geodude," Brock said, looking a little smug. "The one from Kanto is a Rock- and Ground-type. Electric-type moves have no effect!"

Sophocles was annoyed with himself. How could he have forgotten about regional variants? It wasn't like him to miscalculate a match-up that way.

"Sophocles, you just leave everything to

us," Lillie advised. "Snowy, Powder Snow!"

Snowy took a deep breath and sent a blast of Powder Snow to the other side of the arena.

"Geodude! Gyro Ball!" Brock yelled.

"Geo-dude!" The Rock Pokémon made fists and began to spin at great speed. When the Powder Snow hit, Geodude overwhelmed Snowy's move.

"Yeah! Awesome!" Ash cried.

"Dude." Geodude looked proud.

"But ..." Sophocles stammered, confused. "Gyro Ball's an attack move, isn't it?"

"It can be used this way, as a defensive move, depending on how you train with it," Brock explained.

"I've never read about that," Lillie confessed. "Gym Leaders! They're the best!"

"Brock's no pushover," Sophocles said.

"I once had this challenger – during our battle, he taught me how to think outside the box," Brock told them.

Ash looked up when he heard that. He was pretty sure Brock was talking about him!

"I hope you all agree," Professor Kukui said, "Pokémon battling is amazing!"

The Pokémon School students all

murmured with agreement. "With all the Pokémon types, moves and training styles, the kinds of battles a Trainer can have are completely limitless," Professor Kukui went on.

"You also have to know your opponents' Pokémon well, so you can avoid the silly mistake I just made," Sophocles reminded everyone. Togedemaru and Sophocles laughed.

It was just a matter of time before they'd see whether Kiawe and Ash would also make silly mistakes in their big battles. Ash just knew that he wanted to battle well. He wanted to show his friends how much he had learned since he had left them and his hometown.

CHAPTER 9

BROCK VS. KIAWE

"So, Ash and Kiawe, you are next!" the professor said.

"Professor," Kiawe began, his fist clenched with determination. "I want a no-holds-barred Pokémon battle with Brock!"

"Me too," agreed Ash, "but with Misty!"

"You think you'll win?" Misty questioned.

"That'll be the day."

"You may regret this, Kiawe," Brock said.

Professor Kukui had not planned on anyone having one-on-one battles, but Brock and Misty seemed game. Brock's battle with Kiawe would come first.

"I'll be the referee!" Misty volunteered. "This battle is one-on-one. The battle will be over when either side's Pokémon is unable to continue."

"I warn you," Kiawe said. "I'm confident about my strength."

"Happy to hear that!" Brock commended him. "What a Gym Leader looks for is how Trainer and Pokémon combine strengths! That's even more important than winning."

"Which raises my confidence even more," Kiawe replied. He knew he and his Pokémon made a great team.

"Turtonator, let's go!"

"Here's my partner. Come out!" Brock shouted, throwing his Poké Ball straight up.

Steelix burst from the ball with a grumbly growl.

"It's so big," Kiawe said in awe.

"It's Steelix!" Ash announced.

"Steelix. The Iron Snake Pokémon," Rotom shared. "A Steel- and Ground-type. Heat from deep underground strengthens its hide and the pressure gives its body a toughness harder than metal."

"Let's see ..." Sophocles began to strategise using one of his devices. "Steel-type Pokémon are weak against Fire-types, which means ... Turtonator has the advantage."

"But wait," Lillie said. "Fire-type Pokémon are weak against Ground-type moves, so you could also say Steelix has the advantage."

"Then that means they're evenly matched!" Sophocles deduced.

"Brock! Kiawe! I wanna see a great battle out there!" Ash yelled to his friends.

"All right. Battle begin!" declared Misty.

"Turtonator, now! Use Flamethrower!" said Kiawe. Turtonator shot a blast of flame from its snout.

"Steelix, use Gyro Ball!" Brock called out. He chuckled a little and said, "More thinking outside the box."

No one could believe it when Steelix's Gyro Ball dissolved Turtonator's flames, right before their eyes.

"All right, Steelix, Bind. Let's go!" cried Brock.

The Steel- and Ground-type Pokémon sprang forward and wrapped itself around

Turtonator like a constricting snake!

"Turtonator, Shell Trap!" Kiawe shouted.
With incredible force, Turtonator broke
free, sending Steelix flying.

"Hey! Not bad!" Brock said.

"Not so bad yourself!" Kiawe responded.

The two opponents swapped moves, back
and forth, both showing incredible strength.

After a while, Kiawe realised they needed
to try something new. "We can't win

this with a prolonged battle," he said to Turtonator, "so let's finish this off quickly with a Z-Move!"

The Z-Move was Kiawe's secret weapon. Only Trainers from the Alola region had earned the right to do Z-Moves.

"All right! From what I hear, Z-Moves make use of all your power!" said Brock. "Then we'll counter that with all our power! I'm not called Brock the Rock for nothing, you know!"

Ash could hardly contain his excitement. What did Brock have planned?

"Time for Mega Evolution!" Brock announced, pulling out a special pendant. When he held out the pendant, there was a flash of light, and Steelix began growing before their eyes.

Mega Steelix was much bigger, with a

metal mane and gleaming crystal spikes. It roared.

Kiawe watched in awe. "Mega Evolution?" he murmured in disbelief.

"It's Mega Steelix!" Ash declared.

"Brand-new data!" Rotom Dex quickly began recording all the information.

"But how?" Mallow wondered. "Steelix got so much bigger!"

"That's amazing!" Lana agreed.

They were all curious about Mega Evolution, so Professor Kukui offered an explanation. "Mega Evolution is a phenomenon used in battle when a Pokémon's and its Trainer's hearts join as one. It's quite a remarkable thing to see."

"I've heard about Z-Moves," Brock said to Kiawe. "Show me one!"

"Right! And we'll win with it!" Kiawe said

with certainty. "Turtonator, let's go!" Kiawe and Turtonator began a sequence of moves that they completed in unison. They looked like they were moving as one. "The zenith of my mind, body and spirit! Become a raging fire and burn!" Turtonator grunted with effort. "Inferno Overdrive!" Kiawe commanded.

Turtonator shook with effort as it built a mighty blast of fire. It heaved the flames at Steelix in one fluid motion.

Brock assumed a shielding stance and Mega Steelix stood confident.

"What happened?" Kiawe asked after the move was finished.

"How could Mega Steelix withstand a Z-Move?" Ash questioned. All the Pokémon School students were stunned.

"That Z-Move had an incredible amount

of power!" Brock said to Kiawe. "It definitely affected Mega Steelix! But Turtonator wasn't able to go that one last step!" Then Brock declared Mega Steelix's final move. "Use Stone Edge!"

With a mighty grunt, Steelix set off a series of crystal spikes that tunnelled underground and then shot out of the

arena floor. They erupted in a line aimed right at Turtonator.

"Turtonator! Use Dragon Tail!" Kiawe directed at the last second, but it was too little too late. "Turtonator!" he called out.

"Turtonator is unable to battle!" Misty announced. "So Steelix wins!"

"Kiawe lost!" Mallow said, not believing it.

"And all that after Kiawe and Turtonator worked so hard," said Lillie.

"Gym Leaders are strong," Lana pointed out.

"This data will never EVER be deleted!" Rotom claimed, still hyped up from the battle.

"What was that?" Sophocles asked, looking out at the arena. Something had happened to Steelix.

"After a battle, Mega-Evolved Pokémon

return to normal," Professor Kukui explained.

"That was great work, Steelix!" Brock said, pulling out his Poké Ball. "Thanks!"

"Turtonator, you OK?" Kiawe asked, patting the Blast Turtle Pokémon on the head. It was a sweet moment … until Marowak came by and whacked them both with its bone.

"Maro, maro, wak-wak-wak!" Marowak was not happy about the loss.

"Marowak!" Brock scolded. "I know how frustrating losing can be, but you should praise them for their work!"

"Maro." The Bone Keeper Pokémon still wanted to pout more.

"What did you think?" Professor Kukui asked his students. "Tell me."

"I loved it! I was on the edge of my seat!"

Lillie confessed.

Everyone agreed with Lillie. They all thought Pokémon Gym battles were the best!

"Misty, I'm next, don't forget!" Ash said.

"Who, me?" Misty asked. "Forget? Never! You're next! Promise!"

The whole Pokémon School crew held

their breaths. Ash against his old travelling companion and the Cerulean City Gym Leader, Misty – this was going to be good!

CHAPTER 10

MISTY VS. ASH

As Misty was taking her place for her battle with Ash, she pushed a button on a remote control. At once, the Gym arena began to change.

"Whoa," Ash murmured. The floor of the arena sank into the ground and filled to make a deep pool of water. "That's so awesome!" Ash exclaimed. "A Water-type Pokémon battlefield! When you say Cerulean City Gym, it's gotta be water!"

"The field changes with whatever Pokémon are battling on it!" Misty said with a laugh and a hint of warning in her voice.

Kiawe wasn't sure why Ash was so excited. "Does Ash realise that he's just been put at a disadvantage?" he asked Sophocles.

"Where is his Pokémon supposed to stand?" Sophocles wondered.

"I got this covered!" Ash assured his friends. "Pikachu, you're up!" Without a pause, Pikachu leaped out to the rock bridge that ran around the edge of the pool.

"I figured it would be Pikachu!" Misty said.

"Yeah! You know us," Ash admitted.

"Since Misty uses Water-type Pokémon, an Electric-type like Pikachu has the advantage!" Rotom announced to everyone.

"Misty versus Ash! The rules remain the same," Brock declared. "One-on-one!"

"Now the other internationally known beauty!" Misty announced. "Go, my one and only!" She threw her Poké Ball up with a twirl, and a giant Pokémon sprang out with

a deafening roar. Pikachu shuddered.

"It's Gyarados!" Ash yelled.

"Yes, Gyarados, the Atrocious Pokémon," Rotom confirmed. "A Water- and Flying-type. Rumours exist of a town that made Gyarados angry. That town was burned to the ground in one night, leaving no trace!"

Rotom quivered as it told the story, but Brock was not fazed. "Gyarados versus Pikachu!" he said. "Begin!"

"Pikachu! Use Thunderbolt!" Ash directed and Pikachu instantly geared up and shot a bolt toward Gyarados.

"All right, Hydro Pump!" said Misty and Gyarados's water stream met Pikachu's bolt in the middle, cancelling it out.

"See that? Water-type moves can stop Electric-type Pokémon," Misty commented.

"Does not compute!" insisted Rotom.

"Does not compute!"

Ash wasn't going to give up that easily. He knew Pikachu wouldn't either. "Use Quick Attack!" he cried.

Pikachu made a direct hit in the Atrocious Pokémon's face, knocking it over. But Gyarados was too strong to stay down for long.

"Rain Dance," commanded Misty. "GO!" Gyarados reared up to its full height, and a cloud formed around its head. The cloud darkened and grew until it filled the arena and then it started to rain.

"But – how can it rain in here?" Mallow wondered out loud.

"It feels so good," said Lana.

"Don't worry, Pikachu!" Ash said to his partner. Pikachu went ahead and started building up an Electro Ball.

"Gyarados, use Hurricane!" Misty called.

Just as Pikachu shot Electro Ball across the arena with a fierce swat of its tail, Gyarados used Hurricane to knock the attack off target with a gust of damaging wind. Pikachu went spinning to the ground.

"That sure packed a lot of power!" Kiawe noted.

"How about that, Ash? There's nowhere for you to run," Misty chided.

"Using Hurricane in the rain was a good move for Misty! It even cancelled out that Electric-type move that could've caused damage," Professor Kukui said. "So that's Misty's plan to defeat Pikachu."

"Pikachu, are you OK?" Ash asked.

"Pika!" Pikachu was still in battle mode.

"Feast your eyes, Ash!" Misty said, flashing a piece of jewellery that was looped around her ponytail. It took Ash a moment to realise it was a pendant – like Brock's. "Looks great on me, don't you think?"

"You've got one, too?!" Ash said with a gulp. Misty had the pendant to help Gyarados evolve to be even more ferocious?

"Strong, valiant and powerful!" Misty twirled as she spoke in a dramatic voice. "Now, my beautiful blue sweetheart! Mega Evolve!"

Gyarados roared as it transformed, its fins growing longer, its body growing thicker and its expression turning nastier. Mega Gyarados meant business.

"Hey, Misty, this is fun!" Ash yelled to his friend. Pikachu was just as determined.

"Sure is!" Misty agreed. "Now use Hydro Pump!"

Mega Gyarados used Hydro Pump and it sent a tidal-wave-sized blast of water at Pikachu. It knocked the Mouse Pokémon into the pool.

"You're not getting away!" Misty called out to Pikachu. "Use Crunch!" she told her Pokémon.

Mega Gyarados dived into the water with a splash.

Pikachu swam to the edge and began to run across the land bridge. Gyarados was right behind, smashing into the bridge, crumbling it to pieces. "Pikachu, use Iron Tail!" Ash cried.

"It won't work from that posture," Sophocles commented as Pikachu kept running.

"Now jump on Gyarados!" Ash shouted. "Quick, use Iron Tail!"

"Pika, pika, pika, pika." Pikachu bounded on to Mega Gyarados's back. The Mouse Pokémon panted as it ran with all its might, nearing the other Pokémon's monstrous head. Once there, Pikachu used Iron Tail.

"Look at that!" Mallow cheered. "A direct hit!"

Mega Gyarados collapsed in the water, but Ash knew the battle wasn't over.

"You two always were good!" Misty said.

"Here it comes! One more time!" Ash said

to his battle partner.

"Hurricane, go!" Misty shouted, and Mega Gyarados rose from the water, conjuring a rainy cyclone that spiralled towards the ceiling. It picked up Pikachu and the Mouse Pokémon disappeared in the gusty cloud.

"Use Thunderbolt," Ash directed. Pikachu sent the charge through the spinning cloud, but nothing happened.

"That's a Rain Dance and Hurricane combination! Not a single challenger in my Gym has ever broken through it!" Misty bragged.

"That was nice of you to let me know," Ash replied, feeling more confident. "Thanks, Misty! Breaking through stuff like that is what makes battling awesome!"

"What are you talking about?" Misty questioned.

"Hey, Pikachu!" Ash cried. "Can you hear me?"

"Pika, pika!" the little yellow Pokémon replied.

"Climb up the Hurricane!" Ash yelled.

"Does not compute! Does not compute!" Rotom Dex repeated.

But Ash was more sure than he'd ever been. If Pikachu couldn't break through the Hurricane, the Mouse Pokémon would need another way out. "Use Quick Attack and then climb up the electricity!" Ash directed.

"Electric platforms!" Professor Kukui yelled when he figured out what Ash had planned.

They all watched the intense, spinning cloud and waited. At long last, Pikachu shot out of the top.

"It worked!" Kiawe and Sophocles cried, both amazed.

"Uh-huh," Brock said. "That's Ash for you."

"I think it's time for a Z-Move! Let's go, Pikachu!" Ash called out.

"Pika!" Ash's battle partner was ready and willing.

Ash and Pikachu began their Z-Move

sequence, gaining flow and power.

"All right, here we go with FULL POWER, NOW!" Ash called out. "Use Gigavolt Havoc!"

Pikachu focused all its power. It crackled with energy and threw a massive electric pulse right at Mega Gyarados.

The Atrocious Pokémon dropped into the pool.

"Gyarados is unable to battle! Pikachu is the winner!" Brock announced.

"Way to go! You did it, buddy!" Ash was so proud of the way he and Pikachu had battled!

"That was an amazing battle, Gyarados!" Misty said to her battle partner as she held up the Poké Ball. She turned to her opponents. "I think you've got a bit stronger, Ash."

Ash appreciated the compliment, especially coming from Misty. "I've gotta agree with you," he replied.

"But that little kid inside of you still stays just the same," Misty added.

"Little kid inside of me?!" Ash repeated, trying to figure out what Misty meant.

"We're talking really little," Misty continued.

"Now, now," Brock said, bringing the teasing to an end.

"Wasn't that amazing?" Mallow said.

"Yes!" Lillie answered at once. She was really fired up by the whole Gym battle scene.

"Misty's skill with Water-type Pokémon is so inspiring!" Lana added with admiration.

"I'm sure this battle conjured up all kinds of emotions!" Professor Kukui said to his students. "Treasure this experience, and when you're back in Alola, keep it with you!"

"Here," Misty said, handing replica badges to the students she had battled. "They're not real, but they'll remind you of today."

"This is so great," Mallow said, examining the design on the badge. "Thanks a lot!"

"Cerulean is the colour of water!" Lana

noted. "A beautiful blue!"

Brock had given his opponents keepsake badges, too.

"I never would guess that it's a fake," Sophocles said.

"I'll win a real battle next time we meet," Kiawe said with confidence. After his battle with Brock, he looked more ready than ever to devote himself to training.

"You're welcome to try," Brock replied. Even though he was now studying to be a Pokémon doctor, he had not lost his battling abilities from his days of being the Pewter City Gym Leader!

"Misty, do you mind if we come back again?" Lana asked.

"Any time!" Misty said, feeling glad that everyone had had such a good experience at her Gym.

"I just had a great idea," Professor Kukui said. "I'd like to add the Pokémon League as part of Alola's great traditions."

"I think that's a marvellous idea," Professor Oak said.

"And some badges would fit the bill-Lillipup!" Principal Oak agreed, adding another Pokémon pun for good measure.

"That was a lot of fun," Brock said.

"It really felt like old times," added Misty.

"Now it's your turn to come and visit me in Alola!" Ash said to his former travelling companions.

"Count on it, Ash!" Misty and Brock answered together.

"I will!" Ash really meant it. It would be hard to say goodbye to his old pals if he didn't believe he would see them again soon. He had almost forgotten how much he, Misty and Brock had shared. That time had been so early on in his own adventure and he had come so far.

He really loved learning at the Pokémon School. He felt like he grew in his Pokémon knowledge every day. But the time he spent with Misty and Brock was when it all began for him. It was the foundation for everything he knew and loved about Pokémon. He would never forget that time, and he would never forget them. They would always be part of his journey to become the best Pokémon Master he could be!

The End

FIND OUT HOW ASH AND FRIENDS'
ADVENTURES ON ALOLA BEGAN IN

THE POKÉMON SCHOOL

READ ON FOR A SNEAK PEEK ...

"Yippee! Whoo!" Ash yelled. "AWESOME!"

Ash grinned as he gazed out at the wide, blue ocean. He felt a splash of water on his face. Melemele Island, one of several islands in the Alola region, was the perfect place for a holiday! He had Pikachu, his best friend and beloved Pokémon, on his shoulder. The island sun was warm and bright. What could be better?

The answer: zipping over the waves while riding a super cool Sharpedo! Sharpedo was the famous Alola Pokémon jet ski. Instead of a machine with a motor, it was a fabulous Water- and Dark-type Pokémon with super speed.

"Full throttle, Sharpedo!" Ash directed. With several strong flips of its powerful tail, Sharpedo zoomed ahead.

This thrilling Sharpedo ride was just one of the amazing activities Ash could enjoy

on Melemele Island. The Alola region was a tropical paradise, and it had all kinds of unique Pokémon. Even though Ash and his mum were on holiday, he was still thinking about Pokémon.

Ash loved nothing more than encountering new Pokémon. It was his goal to become a Pokémon Master. He had travelled to many regions on his quest to compete at top Pokémon Gyms, but he already knew that his time in Alola would be special.

While Ash and his mum were on Melemele Island, they had an important task. Professor Oak, the famous Pokémon Professor who lived in Ash's hometown in the Kanto region, had asked them for a favour. Professor Oak needed them to deliver a Pokémon Egg to his cousin, Samson Oak. It was a mysterious Egg, and Ash knew it was a very important job.

To get to Samson Oak, Ash and his mum took a taxi. But it wasn't just any taxi.

"My first Pokémon taxi!" Ash declared from the comfortable seat of a cart pulled by a strong Tauros. "This is the best EVER!"

Ash was thrilled. Pikachu made a happy squeak, and the Tauros replied with a friendly grunt. Also along for the trip was Mr. Mime, Ash's mum's Pokémon companion. Mr. Mime, a Psychic- and Fairy-type Pokémon, had actually won the tickets for their big island getaway!

"Here in the Alola region, we use the power of Pokémon to go anywhere and everywhere," the taxi driver explained.

"We refer to these Pokémon as Ride Pokémon. When you travel on land, you take a Land Ride Pokémon. When you want to fly, you take an Air Ride Pokémon. On water, a Water Ride Pokémon."

Ash found it all fascinating. He loved learning new Pokémon facts!

His mum was more interested in the exotic fruit at the local market. She wanted to buy some berries, so the taxi driver pulled Tauros to a stop.

As Ash got out of the cart, he noticed something out of the corner of his eye. It wasn't fruit.

"It's a Pokémon," Ash murmured, rushing over to investigate. The Pokémon was halfway underground, with its tan-and-orange striped head poking out. "So cool!

I wonder what its name is?"

Ash leaned down, and the Pokémon reached out and pinched his nose with its strong pincer-like jaws.

As soon as the Bug-type Pokémon let go, it dived underground and dug an escape tunnel. "OK, let's catch it, Pikachu!" Ash cried, holding his sore nose.

In an instant, the two friends had rushed off into a nearby forest, leaving the market – and Ash's mum – far behind. They raced after the speedy Pokémon.

However, once they were deep in the forest, the Pokémon had too many places to hide. Tall, leafy trees rose high overhead, and lush plants grew all over the forest floor.

"Guess we missed it," Ash said, panting

to catch his breath. Ash looked up and realised that he didn't know where he was. He thought about his mum. "Where were we supposed to take that Egg again?"

The shadows of the forest were a great place to hide. A mysterious Pokémon with large, curved wings floated high in the branches, watching Ash and Pikachu. It stayed out of sight.

Just then, another Pokémon appeared. It was almost twice as tall as Ash and nearly three times as wide. And it was very, very pink. "Oh, wow," Ash said with a gasp.

"Pika!" Pikachu chirped in agreement.

The pink-and-grey Pokémon began to wave its large, log-like arms.

"Look, it's waving!" exclaimed Ash, approaching slowly. "You sure are cute."

The Pokémon appeared to be walking towards them with a friendly grin. Then suddenly it began to whirl around, breaking tree limbs with its gigantic paws. It let out an angry, high-pitched squeak.

"Move it!" Ash yelled, and he and Pikachu ran with all their might. They leaped over bushes and dodged trees until they came to a small clearing.

"What was that thing?" Ash wondered out loud. The super-sized Pokémon had seemed so happy to see them at first.

Luckily, Ash didn't have to worry about it for long. It was only seconds before another Pokémon distracted him. He noticed a Charizard flying high above – with a person on its back!

"That must be an Air Ride Pokémon," Ash said. "That's awesome! Pikachu, let's follow it!"

Ash and Pikachu chased after the Fire- and Flying-type Pokémon. They soon emerged from the trees.

Ash stopped and took in the sight. Before him was a large field with a track around it. There were several grand buildings with thatched roofs and outdoor walkways. The grounds also included a lake and lots of tall palm trees. It was beautiful! And the best part? There were Pokémon everywhere.

Ash stepped forwards in awe. He didn't look before he crossed the track, and three racing Tauros came barrelling full steam ahead, nearly trampling him!

A girl with long blonde hair hurried towards him. "Are you OK?" she asked, worried. Pikachu rushed forward to check on him, too.

Ash laughed it off as he stood up. "Actually, I'm good at dealing with Tauros. See, I've caught some."

Soon, all the Tauros and their riders joined them, too. They all looked concerned.

"What is this place?" Ash asked.

"It's the Pokémon School," said a girl named Mallow.

"The Pokémon School," Ash repeated slowly. "Wow!"

READ *THE POKÉMON SCHOOL* TO FIND OUT WHAT HAPPENS NEXT!

WHICH POKÉMON FROM THE KANTO REGION DID YOU SPOT IN THIS ADVENTURE?

☐ PSYDUCK

☐ GYARADOS

☐ CHARIZARD

☐ **GEODUDE**

☐ **BULBASAUR**

☐ **EXEGGUTOR**

READ ALL THE BRILLIANT

ASH'S BIG
CHALLENGE

POKÉMON PERIL

THE ORANGE LEAGUE

SCYTHER
VS CHARIZARD

RACE TO DANGER

SHOW TIME!

POKÉMON ADVENTURES!

POWER UP PSYDUCK

THE WINNER'S CUP

THE POKÉMON SCHOOL

ALOLAN CHALLENGE

ADVENTURE ON TREASURE ISLAND

OLD FRIENDS NEW BATTLES

Find out about the Pokémon Movies
in the Official Pokémon Ultimate Guide!

Gotta catch 'em all!™

Find information on lots of Pokémon
in this Official Pokémon Encyclopedia!

LOOK OUT FOR THESE OTHER OFFICIAL POKÉMON BOOKS